The Boy Named No

LIANA BROOKS

OTHER WORKS

HEROES AND VILLAINS

Even Villains Fall In Love
Even Villains Go To The Movies
Even Villains Have Interns
Even Villains Play The Hero (books 1 – 3
omnibus)
The Polar Terror

FLEET OF MALIK

Bodies In Motion
Change of Momentum
For Every Action (forthcoming)

SHORTER WORKS

All I Want For Christmas Is A Werewolf
Fey Lights
Prime Sensations
Darkness and Good

Find other works by the author at
www.lianabrooks.com

The Boy Named No

INKLET #46

AMY LAURENS

Inkprint PRESS

www.inkprintpress.com

Print ISBN: 978-1-925825-45-9
eBook ISBN: 9781393444459

www.inkprintpress.com

National Library of Australia Cataloguing-in-Publication Data
Brooks, Liana 1982 –
The Boy Named No
42 p.
ISBN: 978-1-925825-45-9
Inkprint Press, Canberra, Australia
1. Fiction—Science Fiction—General 2. Fiction—Short Stories

First Print Edition: November 2020
Cover photo © Любовь Ганопа via Pixabay
Cover design © Inkprint Press
Interior art © Amy Laurens

THE BOY NAMED NO

Two straight lines of unwanted waifs stood at military attention by their cots. Matron L. R. Rus' heels clicked as she marched down the rows, inspecting hospital corners, checking under the beds for debris, ordering hands held out so she could verify they were properly scrubbed.

The last cot stood alone, blankets folded at the end of the bed where the orderly had placed them the night before. The cot's tow-headed owner was missing.

Again.

Matron Rus scowled. "Justice Saber Rus, get out here this instant!" Not expecting much, she checked under the bed. Nothing. A twinge of clan pride kept her from screaming. He was a Rus; even if he was unwanted, at least he was intelligent.

She eyed his footlocker, then, with practiced ease, overrode his lock code. Shredded uniforms and a shredded gray bag.

Frustration boiling over, she turned to the boy across the aisle. "Where is Justice?"

"He left last night, ma'am."

She scrolled through her mental list of names, trying to place the dark-haired child. Virtuous Shield Pantros. Age six, large for his age and clan. Probably not a full Pantros. "Why, Mister Shield, did you not inform anyone when Justice left?"

"We were told not to make any

noise, ma'am." His dark brown gaze slid upward, watching her.

"You didn't consider the consequences of allowing him to wander away?"

"I did, ma'am. But I can't break the rules, ma'am," he said with infuriating calm.

Matron Rus smiled. "Rebellion by obedience, how very charming. Unit!" she bellowed. "Move out to the cafeteria. You will be fed when Mister Saber joins you."

The children marched out.

With a sigh, Matron Rus collected the tattered gray duffel and dropped it in the carbon recycler. It was always the first thing he destroyed when he threw a tantrum.

She opened the hall closet, looking for a replacement.

"Matron Laura?" a voice interrupted.

"Yes?"

Terssa Camlin Fisher stepped around the corner. "Unit Five just arrived in the kitchen and the little Rondros Pantros girl told me they were waiting for Justice. Where is he?"

"A very good question, Miss Camlin. He's run off again."

Terssa sighed. "The poor dear. He was so upset when the claims list came in yesterday and he wasn't on it."

"He'll never be on the claims list. He's been here for six years and his name has never been listed."

"Little Erinna Sandol Rus was listed this year, and she's nearly nine."

"Erinna's mother brought her to the crèche. The enforcers found Justice wrapped in a bag in a trash can." She slammed the closet door. "Children found in trash cans are not later claimed by their ecstatic family. Now, where are the gray duffels?"

"W-We're out. I can put in an order for more."

Matron Rus grumbled and opened the closet again. "No matter. If the boy didn't shred his things every time he was upset, he wouldn't need a new bag." She pulled out a navy blue bag meant for the children two years younger than Justice. Each year group had their own color, a simple strategy to help the children find their things. Writing names on the inside was the other half of the strategy, and the major sticking point for the little Rus boy.

"I'm going to wait for Justice. Keep an eye on the other children. They'll have to sleep in the cafeteria tonight. I don't want one of his cohorts smuggling him food."

"Yes, Matron."

She returned to the room, lost in thought. *If I were a six-year-old boy, where would I hide?*

Fan-shaped leaves rapping the windowsill drew her attention. The Aral mountains rose in the distance. Thick copses of pine, snow in high summer, and bitter cold tarns. Yes. That would tempt a boy away as the frost cleared from the grass.

Matron Rus took a seat on the boy's spotless footlocker and waited.

Early morning light brightened to noon. Noon warmth faded into early evening. Cold wind rushed down from the mountain heights. As the supper bell rang, she saw one shadow moving amid the lengthening shadows of the trees.

Over the windowsill two white ears appeared. A furry white face with distinctive black stripes followed. Ice-blue eyes glared and whiskers twitched.

Matron Rus stood up and brushed imaginary dust off her skirt. "Well, Mister Saber. Have you finally decided to grace the house with your presence?" She heard his stomach growl.

The little white tiger cub slunk over the windowsill, green burrs clinging to him. Blood matted the fur on his left leg.

"Playing rough were we, Mister Saber?"

Justice sat down in front of her and deliberately licked his paw as if to say she had no control over him.

"Stand up, Mister Saber. I demand an accounting."

The pale blue eyes narrowed. The cub straightened, shoulders arching back. He sat tall and kept growing taller, stretching and flowing out of the white tiger's form and into that of a chubby-cheeked blond boy with dark tan skin and ice-blue eyes.

The burrs fell to the floor with a papery whisper.

"Give me your hand," the matron ordered.

He held out his left hand for inspection.

"Neatly done. Why didn't you shift the injury away before you came in?"

"Didn't wanna," the boy whispered, his voice rasping.

"Hmmmm. Turn." She inspected him head to toe as he pivoted. "No other signs of injury." Although his ribs were showing. "How many times a week are you shifting?"

He shrugged. "Lots."

"You need to eat more if you are changing forms on a regular basis, Justice. If you are shifting more than once or twice a week, I need to know."

Her heart bled for the pathetic little boy. Unwanted. Unheeded.

And, may the ancestors forgive her, so unlovable. Prickly as an urchin. There were days she suspected the boy didn't want to be loved.

He glared at the ground, nose scrunched and lips tightly pursed.

So much for nice.

"Mister Saber, I asked you a question. I expect an answer. How often are you shifting?"

"Lots!" he wailed. The cub's bottom lip jutted out in a pout.

"Daily?"

"What's that mean?"

"Do you shift every day?"

A nod.

"More than once a day?"

Another nod.

Matron Rus sighed. "I expect you're hungry."

No response.

"Mister Rus, are you hungry?"

He shook his head. "I ate something."

"What?"

"I dunno. It hopped."

She blinked. "A rabbit? You ate one of the school rabbits?"

"Not a rabbit!" Justice said, sounding insulted. "It was black, and kinda crunchy. And small."

"A locust?"

"Do they look like giant grasshop-pers?"

"Yes."

He nodded. "It tasted funny."

"You need more than a bug for din-ner. Get dressed and I'll take you down to eat."

The cub nodded eagerly, a smile dimpling his cheeks.

She held out his blue duffel. "Your new bag."

The smile vanished.

"Justice," Matron Rus warned. "Every child at the crèche has their own bag. With name in it."

"It's no' my name," he muttered.

"Your name is Justice Saber Rus. You will write it in the bag, and then you may eat dinner."

He took the bag between thumb and forefinger—and dropped it on the floor.

Turning, the cub went to his locker and pulled out his clothes. He dressed slowly, with a furrowed brow of concentration. He turned to her, jaw set in a defiant line. "My name is not Justice Saber Rus."

"Yes, it is."

"That is your name for me," he said. "It's not my real name. My real name is what my family calls me."

Matron Rus closed her eyes. Would telling him the truth crush him? "Justice, the crèche is your family. We raised you. We named you. We're here for you."

"But you aren't my real family," the cub persisted.

"We're as real a family as you'll ever know."

Pale blue eyes narrowed. Justice growled.

"You are not here because I enjoy these arguments, Mister Saber. No one in the crèche is holding you hostage. We welcomed you in your infancy and gave you a home."

"Because no one else wants me," he whispered.

She sighed and sat on the foot-locker, holding out a placating hand. "Not everyone can keep a child. There are times—"

"When it's okay to wrap a baby in a bag and put them in the trash?"

He'd been listening.

"No, Justice, there is never a time when that is acceptable."

Justice nodded. "I was stolen. A bad man took me from my real family, and threw me away. When my real family finds me I'll have a mommy and a daddy. And sisters. And cousins."

As fanciful delusions went, it wasn't half bad. "No one stole you, Justice."

"Yes they did! My real family wants me! They have a real name for me!"

Matron Rus stood and pulled a pen from her pocket. "We're not arguing. You are here. This is your life. Until such a time as your family arrives to rescue you, your name is Justice Saber Rus. Write it in the bag, and you may eat."

"No." He crossed his arms.

She held the pen out, adamant. "Write. Or you will go hungry."

Justice stood in front of her, bag at his feet, and glared.

The sun set. Night crawled past.

Terssa Camlin Fisher snuck into the room to get someone's stuffed doll so the rest of the unit could sleep down-stairs. Still the cub glared.

As dawn light filtered through the trees, fat tears rolled down the cub's cheeks. He grabbed the pen and sat.

Another hour passed with Justice staring at the bag.

"Write your name," Matron Rus ordered as the breakfast bell rang.

Shaking with rage, Justice opened the bag. She watched the tears fall as he scowled at the white tag. He sniffed. He opened the pen, leaned forward, and scribbled. Then, dropping it all, he stormed out of the room.

Matron Rus waited until she heard his feet running to breakfast before she bent down to inspect the bag. Only one word was inscribed on the tag:

NO

She folded the duffel and put it in Justice's footlocker. Forty years as a crèche matron had taught her patience —and that sometimes, a small bend could break a child. Justice could find his bag now. If he didn't shred it, then they were taking the first step toward healthy adulthood.

And, who knew? Maybe someday the boy named No would find his real family.

THE MAKING OF
THE BOY NAMED NO

Justice Saber Rus, just Ice to most people who have the misfortune of meeting him. The unwanted boy. The forgotten Enforcer of the Felinium. The rogue. The monster.

I wrote the first Ice story in 2007 or so? Maybe 2006? It was tentatively titled *The Demands of Justice* and followed the adventures of Lawful Good Ice Rus as he tracks down a drug dealer and fights off human traffickers.

There was a family of shark-shifters that adopted him, a werewolf socialite he traded barbs and significant looks with, and several corpses. There were drugs, theft, and social injustice. There were very boring passages about moralism and Right versus Wrong.

And there were three other books planned for Ice.

In fact, there were over twelve books plotted out in a series that spanned close to nine hundred years of in-universe history. The series was titled *Vampires In Space* because, yes, it had vampires.

In my mind it was the natural evolution of Urban Fantasy: it was Futuristic Urban Fantasy.

And absolutely terrible.

I wasn't a very good writer yet. Not for fiction, at least. Nearly a decade spent writing for newspapers and scientific journals had severely hampered my imagination, and I was in the self-righteous throws of my early twenties where I was quite certain I knew everything and couldn't imagine how anyone else could believe differently than

I did. And I wanted Ice to be everything I wasn't.

I wanted Ice to be brave, artistic, thoughtful, resilient, loveable…

I wanted a hero who believed in the same things I did and who had the physical strength to actually see justice done. And so Ice was born.

Fey Lights, which you can read the first chapter of over the page, is set in the same universe as *The Boy Named No*, during Ice's adulthood, although Ice doesn't appear in the story.

DOWNLOAD YOUR FREE EBOOK

When you buy a print book from Inkprint Press, we like to say THANK YOU by offering you the ebook for free!

Please head to www.inkprintpress.com/inklets/46/ and the use the coupon INK46LET to get your copy of this Inklet in epub AND mobi today!
(Coupon will only work once.)

Read more by Liana Brooks!

FEY LIGHTS

DARK WATER WRITHED OVER THE SHIP'S deck, a living thing hunting for prey, stinging like acid where it touched bare skin. Jeani stumbled over the guts of her ship, swearing in every language she knew. Her foot fell through a hole in the deck created by the crash. Hot metal gouged her leg as tears ran down her cheeks.

I don't want to die like this. There has to be a way out.

There is *a way out. The same way the water is coming in.*

Running was out of the question. Half-limping, half-swimming through the rising water, Jeani forced herself back to the rear of the ship, navigating by touch and the weak glow of the emergency lights that hadn't burst, back to the gaping wound that was once the engine room and secondary hold. Pressure from the rapid descent into the gravity well and the gushing water warped the frame, creating a strong current. Jeani grabbed the free-fall handle near the emergency door and pressed her free hand to the glowing lock.

Nothing.

She tried yanking the override.

Nothing.

She kicked the door with her good leg.

Pressure sent the door flying inwards at the head of a tidal wave. Jeani gasped for air and went under. Seconds ticked away as she grappled blindly for the next free-fall handle, the current tugging at her.

The hand-hold slipped out of her grip. She pushed up once, bumping her head against the high ceiling of the engine room as she gasped for air. The current swirled under her, pulling her down into the darkness.

Saltwater stung her face. She shuddered as something nipped at her bleeding leg. Ignoring the pain, she clawed at the water until she broke through and gasped in the alien atmosphere. Water crashed over her in the darkness.

Rough, warm sand rubbed against her skin. Sucking in a lungful of the oxygen-rich air, Jeani flipped onto her stomach and pulled herself away from the water. It lapped at her legs, a wayward lover begging her to return.

She laughed as she looked at the strange stars overhead. Her lungs burned, her leg ached, she was shaking with delayed shock, but she was alive. "See, Hothi, I told you I wasn't going to die that easy."

Dominique pushed through the crowd and looked down at the beach.

"Could be a Lander," Gregor said as he adjusted his cap. "Saw the prison ships sailing past this last moon. Could be a Lander," he repeated with a final snort.

A knife waved past Dominique's face, stabbing toward the figure on the beach. "'Twere wedding lights last night. Lit up the sky with fire, set the trees to burning," said Beau.

"'Tain't no fire touched the trees. Trees are fine," Gregor argued. "'Tis a Lander."

"Fey fire," someone said behind him. "Fey burn things with cold fire." A fist hit Dominique's shoulder. "Fey can turn a man's bones to ice. They summon monsters from the deep."

One of the women crossed her fingers and made the sign of the arch to ward off the ill will of the deep dwellers.

"Landers bring plague," Adrian said grimly. He too tapped Dominique's shoulder. "We can't let a Lander near the village."

"We's best shooting it from here," Gregor said.

Another shook his head. "Arrows can't touch fey."

"You volunteering to go down there to slit its throat?" Gregor demanded.

"Such a thing to ask a man! I've got kin, I have."

There was the sound of shuffling feet. A cool sea breeze wrapped around Dominique's legs as the crowd parted. He filled their silence with imagined conversations.

"He's a Lander," one would say in the Silent way of the island-born. *"Got no kin nor woman of his own, does he,"* someone else would murmur.

Dominique kept the snarl he felt forming in his throat from escaping.

"Will you go?" Adrian whispered,

confirming his suspicions. "None will make you, if you say no."

"You'll go?" Dominique asked with a half-smile. Adrian wasn't a bad man. Island born, birthed in the sea, born running on the beach and listening to the waves.

The island-born claimed the waves spoke back to those that listened. The saltwater seeped into their blood so they could hear the thoughts of others like they heard the song of the ocean. Like all the island born, Adrian had no trouble believing every infamy laid against the Landers who lived on the far side of the ocean, in the land of the tyrant.

Adrian shrugged. "Better to slit the Lander's throat on the beach than let it breathe on a child in the village. We'll all die of black blood and fever before the tide is high."

"I'll go," Dominique said, loud enough for his voice to carry to the back of the crowd. "I'll go see to the Lander. I'll send him down to the docks in the south. He can find work there if he likes."

"What if it be fey?" Gregor asked, eyes wide.

Dominique studied the lone figure on the distant sand below, a sad creature sprawled under the hot morning sun. "The fey have a treaty with the Tyrant of Urull. The first tyrant traded his soul for the secrets of the fey lights—wedding lights," he corrected himself, using the island-born term. "The first tyrant lost his mind when the fey showed him the wonders of their world. Men that could turn into dogs. Deep monsters that could walk as men. Women so beautiful that they could suck the soul of a man as he walked past, steal his life with a kiss.

"The tyrants all have made a pact with the fey, traded their subjects to the fey for their favor, but they've never let the fey roam the lands. No fey walk outside the tyrant's gates in Urull. No fey step on the white sands of the islands."

"Maybe this one is outcast," Beau said. "A prisoner, like all the other Landers sent here."

"You've got a leak in your hull," Adrian said, punching Beau in the arm. "You think the tyrant could make a prisoner out of the fey? You think a man could keep one of them under lock and key?"

"But... wedding lights!" Beau lookeded to Dominique for support. "The lights haven't touched our sky in years."

"No one's been out walking in years," Dominique said. "Who was out last night?" He turned and scanned the crowd.

Hardy folk, the island-born. They wore homespun cloth, britches of old sail cloth traded from down the coast, filigree gold necklaces twined around shells and sea gems. All of them came from Lander families at some point in their history, Landers who had either escaped the tyrants, or been banished to a slow death on the distant islands, depending on who you asked.

But the islands were in their blood now. They spoke in Silence, and left him an outcast. The women looked away from him, the older men met his gaze, and one boy blushed. "Tris? Were you out walking last night?"

The boy with dark eyes and a thatch of red hair looked up. "May have been. What's it to you?"

Someone chuckled.

"Explains the wedding lights," Gregor muttered. "You still ought to slit the throat first. That one's not going to give you any answer you'll be wanting."

Keep reading! Head to
[www.lianabrooks.com/
books/short-stories/](http://www.lianabrooks.com/books/short-stories/)
to buy your copy now!

ABOUT THE AUTHOR

LIANA BROOKS was born in California and raised in the American South-West where she developed an appreciation for deserts, cactus, and chilies. She still enjoys driving through the desert sometimes and looking up at the infinity of stars overhead. It's a beautiful place.

When she isn't traveling, Liana enjoys writing science fiction in every form, from sprawling space operas (*Fleet of Malik*) to the antics of a family of superheroes and villains (*Heroes and Villains*).

You can learn more about her and her books at www.LianaBrooks.com.

INKLETS

Collect them all! Released on the 1st and 15th of each month.

Welcome to Dark Dale
LIANA BROOKS

When War Came to Town
A Powers Story
AMY LAURENS

Not Fantasy
AMY LAURENS

Courting the
Winter Prince
LIANA BROOKS

At the Home of the
Winter King
A Winter Faces Story
AMY LAURENS

With
This Ring
AMY LAURENS

Venus &
Seven Reasons I Said No
LIANA BROOKS

OATH KEEPER
AMY LAURENS

FORGET
A Powers Story
AMY LAURENS

NOT QUITE
Cinderella
LIANA BROOKS

ONE BAD MAN
AMY LAURENS

DOUBLE ISSUE
The Claustrophobia
Of Loneliness &
Adam, Be A Star
AMY LAURENS

The
Artist
as a Young Girl
LIANA BROOKS

CONFESSIONS
AMY LAURENS

But For Snow
A Kaliteos Story
AMY LAURENS

The Boy
Named NO
LIANA BROOKS

Anamata
AMY LAURENS

A Wolf FOR
Christmas
AMY LAURENS

www.ingramcontent.com/pod-product-compliance
Lightning Source LLC
Chambersburg PA
CBHW051302190726
48286CB00004B/1231